SUNSHINE STABLES

SOPHIE and the SPOOKY PONY

OLIVIA TUFFIN

ILLUSTRATED BY
JO GOODBERRY

nosy crow

FOR OUR OWN SUPER SOPHIE

First published in the UK in 2021 by Nosy Crow Ltd
The Crow's Nest, 14 Baden Place, Crosby Row
London, SE1 1YW, UK

Nosy Crow and associated logos are trademarks and/or registered
trademarks of Nosy Crow Ltd

978 1 78800 822 8

A CIP catalogue record for this book will be available from the British Library.

Printed and bound in the UK by Clays Ltd, Elcograf S.p.A.

Papers used by Nosy Crow are made from wood grown in
sustainable forests.

3 5 7 9 10 8 6 4 2

www.nosycrow.com

CHAPTER 1

Sophie wiggled her nose a bit, feeling the tickle and prickle of the soft hay. At least it smelt good, she thought, breathing in – like summer and fresh air and ponies. Crouching lower still, she grinned, trying to stop herself from giggling out loud and giving the game away. She could hear Gracie now, chatting away to Willow and Poppy. They were coming into the barn, the door was opening with a creak, the voices getting louder. Now they were walking up to where the sweet meadow hay was neatly stacked, so they could fill their hay nets. It was *perfect* and she was ready.

Three, two, one. "*BOO!*"

Leaping up from behind the bales, hay stuck in her dark curls, Sophie laughed as her friends jumped, dropping their nets.

"Got you!" she said with a chuckle, ignoring their glares. "Again!"

Gracie rolled her eyes and tutted. "Every time!" She said. But she was sort of laughing now and threw a handful of hay at Sophie in response. Not that it would make any difference – it was already all over Sophie's camp T-shirt and jodhs, as well as tangled in her hair.

"Ha!" Sophie said as she joined her friends. "You *should* know by now."

Willow was busy filling her hay net, her glossy brown hair tied back in a ponytail. She was wearing jodhs and a running top that had her name in red letters across the back. Willow ran cross-country races with the town running club and was often in the local paper for her achievements.

"Sophie," she said once the giggles had died down, "have you not finished your stable? We've got to be in the arena in ten minutes! It'll take you *that* long to get all that hay off you!"

"Of course I've finished!" Sophie said airily. She'd quickly swept up the shavings, and got Jack, who lived on-site at Vale Farm, to help her with the rest.

"You know Lainey might get cross if you *haven't* finished the stable, though," Willow replied slightly doubtfully. "You remember what she said at the start of camp? How things had to be done properly?"

"I know, I know!" Sophie said cheerfully. "And it *is* done. Gorse is back in, all happy. Don't worry, I remember the camp rules!"

Sophie had been looking forward to pony camp at Vale Farm, the local riding stables, for *ever.* Lainey was Jack's mum and owned the stables. She had run the camps for a couple of years and they were very popular, especially with children like Sophie who didn't own their own pony but longed to. There were lessons, and a beach ride, and even a camp cookout in one of the fields to look forward to. It was pony heaven! Sophie smiled, remembering the moment her mum had agreed to book her a place at the camp, and she'd leapt about crazily.

"Oh, Sophie." Her dad had smiled once she'd finally calmed down. "Your grandmother would be so happy. It's a shame she's so far away."

Sophie sighed every time her dad reminded her of this. Her grandmother still lived in Nigeria, where her dad had been born and raised. He'd met her mum when he came over to England to study. Her grandmother loved horses and had even kept some in her younger days. She and Sophie spoke regularly – it was always so good to wave to each other on screen. Sophie thought back to their last conversation, when she'd told her grandmother all about the upcoming camp.

"I'll take loads of photos," she had said. "Then you can see how much I've improved."

"Oh, I know you will have," her grandmother replied. "Ponies were always in your blood, Sophie. Your brothers still showing no interest?"

And Sophie had sighed dramatically.

"No," she said. "Still into football, and boring old cricket like Dad. I mean, why stand in a field catching a ball when you could be galloping around it?"

Her grandmother laughed heartily at that. "Maybe they'll come round."

"I doubt it," Sophie replied. "No one cares about horses, apart from you."

When her mum had dropped her off at camp, her older brothers, Samuel and Joseph, had been in the car as well, dressed in their team tracksuits ready for a cricket match, their kit bags jostling for space with Sophie's pony things.

"Is this it?" Samuel had asked, looking up at the stables with a wrinkle of his nose. "Just looks like a farm."

"It's a riding school," Sophie had explained. "The owner competed at Badminton Horse Trials. That's really famous – you have to be super skilled to do that. It's dressage, showjumping and cross-country – a three-day event. Why don't you come and look?"

"Nah, we're good here," Joseph said, flicking through his phone as he read the latest football results. He and Samuel were *obsessed* with knowing which team was winning at what. "I don't want to be late for cricket. And, anyway, riding's not actually a *real* sport, is it?"

"Of course it is!" Sophie cried. "If it wasn't, it wouldn't be at the Olympics, would it?"

"But how much skill do you need to just sit there?" Samuel grinned.

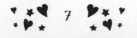

Sophie had rolled her eyes, letting herself out of the car. There was no point trying to explain. No one *really* listened, or got her love of horses, like her grandmother.

But it was her mum who'd found Vale Farm, and Lainey, about a year before. Her grandmother had insisted on paying for the lessons. Sophie had thrown herself into learning, and had been on the waiting list for camp for what had felt like for ever. She'd asked her mum to sign her up as soon as she'd heard about it, after a lesson one day. And, now she was here, she was going to enjoy every minute!

Even better, after learning to ride on Henry, a sweet but steady cob, she had been paired with Gorse, who she'd loved from the first moment she set foot in the yard. Gorse was a beautiful Exmoor pony. He was bay with rich dapples running over his strong shoulders and a lustrous

black mane and tail. His eyes
were ringed with a lighter
brown, which Lainey had
explained was known as
"toad eye".

Sophie had laughed, wrinkling her
nose. She'd come to see Gorse after her
lesson a few weeks earlier. "It doesn't sound
very nice for such a beautiful pony."

"No," Lainey had agreed with a chuckle.
"But he's a fantastic example of an Exmoor."
She had given Gorse a friendly pat. "Did
you know, he was champion at the
Exmoor Breed Show? It was a wild, windy
day on top of the moor and by the end of it he
had so many sashes on you could barely see him.
He loved to strut his stuff in the ring."

"Do you think he misses those days?" Sophie
had asked, and Lainey had smiled.

"No," she said. "I think he prefers his life now, keeping busy with the camps, loads of people admiring him, and mischief to be made!"

Sophie had a feeling she would get on with him very well! Luckily, it was as though Lainey had read her thoughts, and the handsome Exmoor pony was hers for the week.

Quickly stuffing her hay net, Sophie skipped happily back out to the yard. The warm sunshine spilled over the cobbles, and Mini, Lainey's tame pet sheep, was sunning herself next to an old stone trough. Mini was an escape artist with real character, and Lainey had told the children it was easier to let her roam around, rather than trying to shut her in. Sophie's family had a cat and a dog, but there was no way they'd fit a sheep in the garden! She loved spending time at Vale Farm with all the animals.

"Uh…" Gracie, next to her, interrupted her thoughts. "Wasn't Gorse supposed to be in his stable? You said you'd put him back…"

Sophie looked, and blinked twice. Gorse was standing outside the door of a pretty grey mare a few stables down, his ears pricked as they nuzzled their soft noses. Giving a little snort, he then headed straight towards the open door of the feed room. Immediately, Sophie could see what had happened.

"Whoops!" she said. "I forgot to put his kick bolt on. Isn't he clever?" she added fondly.

"He knows how to undo his top latch."

"He sure is," Poppy said. "But you'd better get him before Lainey sees!"

"Too late," Willow muttered. "She's over there…"

Sophie bit her lip. At camp, each girl and boy was responsible for looking after their own pony.

"Sophie?" Lainey called, coming towards the girls with a little frown. "Did you forget Gorse's kick bolt? You know what I said about him – he doesn't miss a trick. You've got to be careful."

Sophie's face fell. It was quite funny that Gorse was clever enough to escape, but it wouldn't do to have him get into the feed room, where he'd undoubtedly break into all the bins.

"Sorry, Lainey."

Grabbing Gorse's dark green head collar from the hook outside his stable, Sophie caught the pony. She gave him a huge hug and he gave her a whicker in return.

"Well done," Lainey nodded. "But, Sophie, you need to concentrate. I can't have any accidents happening because of you being careless. We might have to have a serious think about your lessons. It might do you good to miss one or two so that you can practise some stable management instead."

Sophie nodded and led Gorse back to his stable. Lainey very rarely told anyone off so she knew it was serious, and the threat hung in the air. Sophie bit her lip, thinking about what her grandmother would say. The thought of any riding time being lost was enough to snap her out of her joking mood, for a few minutes at least!

CHAPTER 2

"Right, everyone!"

Lainey had gathered all the camp members in the stable yard, each holding on to their ponies. They were heading out on a hack, a ride across the countryside surrounding the farm. There was Gracie and her piebald pony Bobby, who was grumpily surveying his surroundings. *He is such a crosspatch*, Sophie thought, glad she wasn't Gracie. Gorse was far more cheerful! Then Poppy and Henry, one of Vale Farm's long-standing resident ponies, who'd taught hundreds of children to ride. Jess had a lovely grey called Merlin, and Amina rode little Nutmeg, who was an amazing jumper. Willow rode Luna, who was fast and suited her perfectly.

"Make sure you all check your girths," Lainey continued, fastening her riding hat. "I'll be coming on Bertie," she said. Lainey's retired event horse, Major Green, was a famous Badminton winner who was known as Bertie at home, "and Jade will join us with Sox."

As if on cue, Jade, the assistant instructor at Vale Farm, led Sox out of his stable. He was a big dapple grey with wise eyes. But today there was something different about him.

"Come on, Sox," Jade frowned, giving the horse a pat as she led him forward. Sox's head was held high, and he gave a loud whinny. One or two of the camp ponies shuffled in interest as Sox high-stepped past, giving a snort. He was normally so calm and quiet.

"Sox," Lainey said curiously as she hopped up

into Bertie's saddle, "what's got into you?"

"I don't know." Jade shook her head. "He's been in a funny old mood all morning. Hopefully a hack out will settle him down."

"Oh," said Lainey. "Perhaps it's the grass. We've had a warm spell and some rain recently, so the grass will be growing again," she explained to the camp members. "It can send them a bit crazy."

Jade nodded. "Hopefully just the grass," she said, deftly swinging herself up into Sox's nut-brown saddle and gathering up his reins as he spooked at an imaginary object.

"Come on, silly sausage," she said fondly, nudging him on. "Let's be sensible now. Look, the ponies are ignoring you."

But Sox seemed to be looking at something, something that wasn't there.

"Ooh," Sophie said with a grin to her friends. "Maybe he can see ghosts!"

"Well," Lainey said, overhearing. "They do say horses have a sixth sense. They can sense and see things that we can't."

"Oh, don't," Poppy said with a groan. "I'll never sleep if I think about that. It's hard enough dealing with normal things that spook ponies, like flappy plastic bags and birds flying out of hedges, let alone ghosts." She reached over to pat sweet Henry. "Not that I have to worry about that with you, boy."

"I'm sure it's just the grass." Lainey smiled, but Sophie wondered if she could detect the tiniest note of something in her voice. Doubt? She wasn't sure.

It was soon forgotten, though. The riders headed out of the big gates, turned right and down the lane. There were endless bridleways and fields to explore.

"It sounds *boring*," her brother Samuel had said

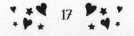

the last time she had tried to explain it to him. "Just plodding around on a horse."

"It's not," Sophie had retorted. "I bet if you gave it a chance, you'd see!"

"Ugh," he had laughed, pretending to waft away an imaginary bad stench. "And smell like poo? No thanks."

And Sophie had stuck out her tongue and left him to it. She loved her brothers, but it upset her when they teased her, not that she ever showed it. *How could it be boring?* she thought, looking at the open countryside from between Gorse's pricked ears.

Sophie and her family lived in one of the new builds on the edge of town. They were friendly with all their neighbours and her mum and dad often had people around, her brothers' friends trailing in after school, muddy sports kits dumped in the hall. But Sophie liked to escape to her bedroom, plastered with posters from *Pony* magazine,

where she had the best views out across the houses and towards Vale Farm and the fields where she was now riding. She'd dreamed of this!

"Oh, Gorse!" She leant forward and gave the little Exmoor a pat, quickly checking no one could hear her. She was Sophie the joker and it wouldn't do for the others to see her being serious! "I wish my brothers understood how horses make me feel. Like you, you see the *real* me."

Gorse gave a snort and Sophie smiled. At home she had to be louder, funnier, wilder than her brothers to get noticed above the constant chatter about matches, and goals, and cricket runs. But she didn't have to be loud with Gorse. She felt as though he understood her, without her even having to say a single word.

CHAPTER 3

The camp members enjoyed the most wonderful canter up through a big grass field. Gorse was surprisingly speedy, considering he was a stockily built pony. His thick black mane flew out behind him, and Sophie grinned as he put his head lower and thundered on. He was a bit cheeky sometimes, but Sophie felt really safe riding him. Ahead of them, Lainey slowed Bertie down to a bouncy trot.

Gracie caught up with Sophie and sighed. "That was amazing. You've bonded with Gorse so well."

Sophie gave her friend a sympathetic smile. She knew Gracie was finding her pony, Bobby, tricky.

"He's great," Sophie said. "He's funny."

Looking around, Sophie noted that Sox seemed calmer now. He'd obviously needed a good canter up the hill. Thinking back to what Lainey had said in the yard, Sophie found herself wondering what horses could see that they couldn't. She would have to talk about it with her grandmother next time she rang. She knew her grandmother would have some tales. She giggled to herself, imagining Gorse chatting to a ghost. It certainly didn't scare her like it did Poppy.

It felt like hardly any time had passed when they arrived back at the stable yard of Vale Farm. Kicking her feet out of her stirrups, Sophie wiggled her toes. Jumping down, she quickly untacked, placing the head collar over Gorse's nose and tying him up in the warm sunshine so she could wash him down.

Filling a bucket with water, she got a sponge and set to work, placing the bucket down in front of the little Exmoor. That, she realised, had been a mistake. Grabbing the bucket in between his strong teeth, Gorse picked it up and promptly flung water everywhere, soaking Sophie in the process.

"Oh, Gorse!" Sophie found she didn't mind one bit. After a long hack, it was nice and refreshing! "Now I'll have to go and fill it up again."

Wiping the droplets from her eyes and shaking out her curly hair, Sophie headed back over to the tap. It was next to a little paddock where Mini and the other sheep lived, and where the chicken coop was. There was a lovely old pony in there today – Fable, who belonged to Lainey's daughter, Emily.

Fable was an elderly Welsh Mountain Pony, with the sweetest dished face and a pink snip between her nostrils. Her back was bowed with age and she was almost pure white now, but she still had her cheeky moments. Lainey said they let her get away with loads because of how old she was and how special she was to the family. She was the one pony who *wasn't* used for lessons or camp.

Placing her bucket down, Sophie turned the tap on, and humming to herself, began to think about what prank she could play next. Looking over at the chickens scratching about in the earth, and at Fable munching on the hedgerow, something caught her eye. She frowned and looked closer. That was weird! Moving nearer, the chickens clucking as though they were mildly annoyed at having to get out of the way for her, Sophie crouched down to investigate.

There were some strange marks in the soil, sort of like dog paw prints, as though something had been scratching at the ground. And there was an even stranger mark next to the prints, like something had been dragged along there. Despite the warm sunshine and the cloudless sky, Sophie felt a little shiver run through her. Then she grinned, the thrill of what she had found overriding any slightly spooky feeling. She had to tell her friends!

"The water!" she heard someone shout, and looking up she saw her bucket was overflowing, the water cascading over the cobbles towards her.

"Uh-oh."

Jumping up, Sophie grabbed the full bucket, sloshing water all over her feet as she made her way back to where Gorse was fiddling with his lead rope. He looked sideways at Sophie, as if telling her that had he been left a minute longer, he would have been loose and causing mayhem. Sophie gave him a hug and set to work on washing him down, still thinking about the strange prints.

But once Gorse was sponged off and back in the stable, this time with the kick bolt firmly in place, she couldn't find her friends, who had long finished their chores. Instead, crossing the yard, Sophie met Lainey, who was leading a prancing and snorting Bertie back towards his own stable.

"Goodness me!" Lainey said, looking hot. "Calm down, boy." She sounded both exasperated and amused. "Really, you're far too old to be behaving like this."

Bertie gave another snort and leapt about a bit, ignoring Lainey as she tried to lead him into his stable. His eyes were fixed on something, and he looked really spooked.

"Shall I go and get a feed scoop?" Sophie asked, and Lainey looked up. She seemed surprised, Sophie thought. Perhaps she wasn't used to Sophie being sensible.

"Thank you, Sophie.

Good idea," Lainey said in a relieved voice. "That would be really helpful."

The pony nuts did the trick. Bertie's ears pricked as Sophie ran back, giving the scoop a good shake, and his eyes lit up as he obediently followed her into the stable. But even as Lainey gave him a handful of the nuts as a reward, Bertie still seemed distracted, pausing as if looking or listening for something before resuming his munching.

"Well, I don't know," Lainey said, giving him a pat as she let herself and Sophie out of the stable. "The two biggest on the yard are the two most jittery today!"

"What do you think it is?" Sophie asked curiously.

"Oh, just horses being horses," Lainey said. "Sometimes when one gets spooked, the others follow – herd behaviour." She chuckled. "Bertie should know better, though, at his age."

But Sophie remembered the note of uncertainty in Lainey's voice earlier, when she and Poppy had been talking about ghosts. Was there something else going on?

CHAPTER 4

"What *exactly* do you want us to look at?"

Willow sounded a bit confused. She and the other camp members had just been hanging out in the cool of the camp barn where they slept when Sophie came to find them.

"You'll see!" Sophie hopped from foot to foot. "I saw something earlier, something really weird! Strange paw prints." She grinned at her friends. "Come on! Just come and look for yourselves!"

"Oh, Sophie, I don't know," Poppy said, sounding unsure. "I really don't like the thought of something scary out there. Especially after what Lainey said this morning, about horses seeing things."

"She's only winding us up," Gracie said kindly, giving Poppy a gentle nudge.

"I'm not!" Sophie insisted. "They were like wolf or even bear prints. Or *werewolf*." She flexed her fingers like scary claws. "Maybe that's why Sox was so freaked out!"

"Fine," Jess said, rolling her eyes. "We'll come and see these prints. I bet it was just a chicken!"

Everyone laughed at this, even Poppy. Sophie laughed too, but she knew they weren't. She'd seen them for herself! She'd been trying to come up with the perfect prank, but this was even more fun!

"Come on!" Leading the way, Sophie headed back out into the stable yard and across to the little paddock where the sheep and chickens were.

"So what *are* we looking at?" Willow said, sounding a bit huffy.

"I don't see anything," Gracie said. "See!" She smiled at Poppy. "Told you she was just joking."

Sophie frowned and looked. Where she'd let Gorse's bucket overflow, the water had flowed over the dust, sinking into the dry earth. The sheep were mooching around, and the chickens were scratching enthusiastically at the dampened soil. There were sheep prints and chicken prints and a few Fable hoofprints, but no sign of the strange prints Sophie had seen. They had completely vanished!

"Ha, ha," Willow said. "I *knew* you were having us on. Come on, you've jumped out on us, like, three times in the hay barn so far. All you do is joke!"

Sophie bit her lip. "I'm not having you on!" she said. "I promise you, they were just here. Really weird paw prints – I've never seen anything like them."

"Yeah, yeah." Willow seemed to have lost interest. "Come on, let's finish reading *Pony* magazine."

Feeling a bit deflated, Sophie trudged behind her friends as they headed back to the barn. She *hadn't* been joking at all. She knew what she had seen!

A short while later, with everyone back in the camp barn and crowded round the latest copy of *Pony*, Sophie found her thoughts wandering.

She felt annoyed that no one had believed her earlier. Distracted, and not really that interested in the magazine quiz, she found her eyes drawn to the horseshoe the girls had hung on the barn wall for luck on their first day at camp. Willow had found it underneath the old oak tree in the yard. It had been a talking point, something that had helped the girls bond as they hung it up together.

Frowning and glancing round at her friends, who were totally engrossed in the quiz, Sophie reached up. Unhooking the horseshoe from the nail, she turned it over in her hand, stroking the worn metal. There was some faint writing on the inside, but they'd all been too excited to try to read it at the time.

Squinting, Sophie looked closely at the inscription, tracing the words with her finger. Sophie gazed at the shoe. *Who was the pony behind*

the words? Carefully placing it back on the wall, she headed out to Gorse, giving him a big hug as he whickered in delight at seeing her.

Lainey, passing by with an armful of bridles, stopped and smiled.

"Thanks again for your help," she said. "Bertie's calmed down a bit but, goodness me, what a carry on!"

"That's OK." Sophie patted Gorse, then let herself back out of the stable. Lainey glanced in, and Sophie looked guiltily at the slapdash banks of shavings around the edge and the hastily swept back bed. Henry's stable, next door, was beautifully neat, and Sophie knew Poppy's hard work made her efforts look worse. And it appeared Lainey had noticed too. She gave a little frown.

"I think it would be good for you to do another job for me now," she said in a brisk voice. "I've got just the thing…"

CHAPTER 5

A short while later, Sophie muttered darkly to herself as she pushed a wheelbarrow up the field behind the stables. This was where the ponies spent the late afternoon after lessons, before the camp members brought them back in for the night. There were some other ponies in the field next door, on the other side of a post-and-rail fence, ponies who were not taking part in the week's camp but were having a rest instead. With Vale Farm's camps proving very popular, they needed plenty of ponies so they could all enjoy some weeks off.

Sophie pulled a face as the hill got steeper. She

knew deep down that Lainey had given her the task because she had been shirking her stable duties, and it could have been so much worse – she could have had her riding lessons taken away, especially after Gorse escaped. *Perhaps Lainey had been planning to do that*, she thought, *but then I helped her with Bertie and she decided to give me another chance.* Grabbing the fork, she got to work picking up the poo from around the field, grumbling to herself as she did so.

The barrow started to grow heavy so Sophie put it down and looked around. *Actually, it's quite nice being up here*, she thought. She could see the yard and the sheep and Fable in the little paddock. She couldn't see Gorse but she hoped he was snoozing in the shade

of his stable. Balancing the fork on the barrow and sitting down, Sophie let the warm sunshine wash over her. There was *plenty* of time to finish this boring chore.

Suddenly the peace was shattered. The ponies in the next field all looked up with a startled toss of their heads, a few began trotting nervously around as one whinnied.

"Hey, guys?" Sophie thought she had better go over to the fence, just in case they needed calming down. "What's going on?"

Then she looked up, following the ponies' gaze to the very top of the hill, and felt her heartbeat quicken. There was something there, something in the hedge that bordered the top of both fields. Something *big*. The lower branches were shaking, but it couldn't be the wind as the air was still and warm. Sophie picked up the fork and edged forward. As she drew nearer, she could hear a loud rustling coming from deep within the brambles.

Sophie smiled to herself as she reached the hedge, imagining Poppy in the same situation – she would be *terrified*. But Sophie just felt curious. Crouching down, she held her breath, daring to poke the lower branches with the end of the fork.

"Hello!"

"Aargh!" Leaping into the air, Sophie placed a hand on her chest as something scrambled

through the brambles out of sight. She glared in the direction of the voice. She could practically hear her heartbeat through her camp T-shirt; it was thumping like a drum.

A woman about her grandmother's age was standing on the other side of the hedge. Sophie let out a big sigh of relief. The ponies seemed to recognise the woman and trotted over eagerly to the top gate, where she greeted them with lots of friendly pats. Cautiously, Sophie moved over to the gate too.

"Hello, Star; hello, Tinker. Ella, there's a girl." The woman then noticed Sophie and smiled. "Oh, sorry, dear," she called over. "I didn't mean to startle you."

Sophie smiled back. She *had* been startled, but she was glad it had just been the woman and not something strange!

"That's OK," she said. Then she had a thought.

"Did you see anything just now? Like something in the hedge?"

The woman shook her head.

"No," she said, with a little shrug. "I expect it was my dog, Alfie, sniffing around."

Sophie looked down. The dog was sitting at the woman's feet. He was obviously quite old and also really small, not like her family's big boxer dog. She was pretty certain that whatever had just spooked the ponies wasn't the dog. But what other explanation was there?

"Are you enjoying camp?" the woman asked.

Sophie nodded, wondering how she knew about it.

"Loads," she replied. "It's the best."

"It was a super idea of Lainey's," the woman said with a smile. "I've known her since she was a little girl, and I always knew the stables had big potential. I used to ride the ponies, and we would have people asking to bring their children up for lessons even then. I'm so glad Lainey opened up the yard."

"Wait, did you use to work here?" Sophie asked, her ears pricking up, and the woman nodded, leaning on the gate.

"It's many years ago now, but I still like to walk Alfie up and say hello to all these lovely ponies. It's all very different today, though, with all your high-tech rugs and horse feeds!"

Sophie knew she wasn't going to get the job done quickly now. The woman reminded her of her grandmother, and Sophie asked her question after question. She learned her name was Mary, and she enjoyed her stories of plaiting ponies' manes for gymkhanas, and of jute rugs and bran mashes cooked up on the old stove in the feed room.

"Well!" Mary laughed as they finally finished

chatting. "I must get on with Alfie's walk now." She eyed the barrow as she straightened up. "Looks like you've got work to do too." Then she glanced up at the sky. "It'll be a full moon tonight, so maybe you'll catch a glimpse of dear Rosie."

Now Sophie was *really* intrigued!

"Who?" she asked, the poo picking completely forgotten.

Mary smiled and leant back on the gate, stroking a grey pony who had come up to them. Mary didn't seem in a hurry to leave any more.

"Rosie," she said. "Fable's mum."

Sophie thought of Fable, who'd been grazing out in the little paddock where she'd found the prints.

"Do you know about Fable's past?" Mary asked, and Sophie shook her head.

"No," she said. "Only that Lainey's owned her for years and years."

"Since she was born." Mary gave a small sad smile. "It was almost thirty years ago. I was there." She paused, as if recalling the memory. "Darling Rosie fought so hard but she didn't get to stay long with Fable after the birth. Lainey did so well, bottle-feeding little Fable all through the night for weeks and weeks, and she wasn't much older than you are now."

Sophie gasped. "Rosie died?"

Mary nodded.

"It was so terribly sad," she said. "But she's still around, really, looking after Fable, keeping an eye on the stables and all the ponies and the children. When the moon is high and the nights are clear, sometimes you can see her, just galloping up over the fields. It's nice knowing she's there. She was a lovely pony. Mischievous too, so mischievous. She knew how to open stable doors."

"Oh my," was all Sophie could say. She didn't feel spooked in the slightest. It made her feel special, knowing a bit of the yard's history. And Rosie sounded so like Gorse with her stable-opening abilities!

"Well, I really *must* go now," Mary said with a smile. "Nice to meet you!"

Alfie got up and yawned, and with a wave Mary set off on her way. Sophie headed back to the barrow. She checked her watch and realised she needed to be tacking up Gorse ready for her next lesson in a few minutes. She was sure she'd missed a few poos, but it couldn't be helped, not when she'd just learnt all about Rosie and Fable!

CHAPTER 6

A short while later, Sophie was quickly slipping the bridle over Gorse's furry ears and rearranging the brow-band on his generous forehead. She gave him a kiss. The little Exmoor had given her a merry whinny as she hurried over to his stable with his tack. Sophie's head was still full of the conversation she'd had with the lady in the field.

"Before you all get on," Lainey told the camp members gathered in the stable yard, "I just want to remind you about the camp cookout this evening." She looked around at all the eager, expectant faces with a smile. "We'll be heading out to the big field for a barbecue after you've done your stable chores."

Everyone looked around at each other and an excited murmur ran through the group. The ponies seemed to be picking up on it too, and a few of them jostled around. Leaning forward and giving Gorse a pat, Sophie was struck by a thought. The lady had said they might see Rosie on a full-moon night! They would be out in the big field, so it would be the perfect place to spot her.

It would be a fun evening for telling spooky stories too. For now, though, she just wanted to keep Fable's story to herself. It didn't seem right to tell the tale straight away. It was special, not a joke. And anyway, she had other things she could spook her friends with. She knew the prints had been real, and then there was the strange rustling in the hedge earlier, and the alarm of the ponies!

"Round the corner, inside leg on and ask for canter!" For the next hour, Sophie had to concentrate hard on Lainey's instructions. Lainey had set up a little grid in the arena, and they were jumping the low cross-poles without stirrups, and then without reins, holding their arms out like aeroplane wings. It was right up Sophie's street — fun and a bit daring too. It was a chance to show off her riding skills. With natural balance and rhythm, she found the jumping exercise really easy!

Kicking her feet out of her stirrups, Sophie took her place in the line-up, awaiting her turn. Amina and Nutmeg, a sweet palomino and Welsh Shetland cross, were now jumping through the grid. Amina was grinning happily, her two long plaits flying out behind her, and little Nutmeg was popping over the jumps, tucking her feet up neatly. Jess was waiting next to Sophie on her

pony, Merlin. But Merlin seemed unsettled and wouldn't stand still. He shuffled his feet and flung his head around. It was very similar to how Sox had been behaving before the hack.

"Steady, Merlin," Jess said calmly. She was a brilliant rider and Sophie knew she had loads of horse experience. "There's nothing there."

"Nutmeg!" Looking a little breathless, Amina pulled up the small pony. Nutmeg's tiny ears were pricked forward as far as they could go and her eyes were wide as she flung her head up.

"There's something in that corner she doesn't like!" Amina said, patting Nutmeg as the pony wheeled round, looking down into the bottom corner of the arena.

"That's what Merlin was looking at," Jess said with a little frown. "I really had to work hard to get him past that corner. One minute, fine, then not. So weird."

Sophie looked too. The bottom corner of the arena bordered the little paddock where Fable lived with the sheep and chickens, the same paddock where she had found the prints. There was an old blue barrel on its side, not particularly spooky, and, anyway, it had been there for ever, so the ponies were used to it.

"It's probably whatever made those prints!" she said aloud, and Poppy, who had just joined them, went pale.

"Not that again," she said. "There wasn't anything there!"

Sophie frowned. "I'm telling, you, there was!"

Just you all wait until later, she thought. She would recount what she'd seen in the big field. Then she could tell them what the lady had told her, about Fable and Rosie. She'd save that story for last, because it was the best.

It was now Sophie's turn to jump for the

final time. Patting Gorse's sturdy neck, Sophie gathered up the plaited reins and gave him a nudge. Gorse was forward-going and loved jumping. But as Sophie trotted him down the long side of the arena, it was as though a current of electricity had passed through him. Sophie felt his whole body tense as he tucked his head in and slowed right down, blowing out from his nostrils, his eyes bulging.

"Come on, Gorse!" Lainey called. "Not you too?"

Sophie gave the little Exmoor a determined nudge, trying to get him trotting again, but Gorse was backing away from the blue barrel and the bottom corner of the field. It felt as though he might sink back on his haunches and spin around at any second. It was a bit unnerving, Sophie thought, gritting her teeth. Giving Gorse a scratch on his withers, she nudged him again.

Uttering an exaggerated snort, Gorse high-stepped past the scary blue barrel, practically curving his body round as he stared at it.

"I don't know what's got into you ponies today!" Lainey threw up her hands. "Well done, Sophie – well ridden."

Now they were past the corner, Sophie felt

Gorse relax and they jumped easily through the grid, Sophie's arms out wide again. But there *had* been something there. Sophie was sure of it!

Lainey had another explanation, though.

"It's classic herd behaviour," she said, repeating what she'd told Sophie, as everyone warmed down at the end of the lesson, all avoiding the bottom corner. "Like Sox and Bertie this morning. I expect after Nutmeg spooked, the others all decided to have a silly moment too."

But Sophie *knew* something was up. She'd felt it in Gorse. He hadn't been silly – he really had seen or sensed something. When he was being mischievous, untying himself and throwing his water buckets around, he had a real glint in his eye. But this time, as he'd curved his neck round to stare at the barrel, Sophie had noticed his eyes were different. He had been scared.

The others might be convinced, but she wasn't.

First the prints, and now the ponies acting strangely. And it hadn't been the dog scaring the ponies up in the field, she just knew it. She couldn't stop thinking about Lainey's comment about how horses could see things that humans couldn't. Just what could her gorgeous little Exmoor see, she wondered, giving him a hug. What was going on?

CHAPTER 7

Everyone was talking about the camp cookout as they untacked their ponies. Willow had heard from Jack that Lainey had bought large bags of marshmallows for toasting, and Zoe, Lainey's head groom, had already been up to the big field to set up the campfire.

Emily, Lainey's daughter, strolled by. She tended to ignore the camp members, unlike Jack, who was always hanging around and helping with a cheerful smile. Poppy had told Sophie earlier in the week that Emily didn't like other people grooming or riding the school ponies, even though it was the reason the stables were doing so well. She only really spoke to the girls to point out things that were wrong. So far today, according to Emily, Henry had the wrong boots on to protect his legs when jumping and Nutmeg didn't have the right hay net.

Crossing over to the tap, Sophie watched as Emily gave Fable a big hug. But even the elderly Welsh pony seemed different. She wasn't munching on the grass as usual. Instead her head was held high, her pink nostrils quivering as she gave a shrill whinny. The sheep lifted their heads too, and Mini, the tamest one, gave a long baa. There was *definitely* something in the air.

Sophie opened her mouth to say something, perhaps ask Emily a bit more about Fable's history and whether the ponies regularly got spooked around the full moon, but Emily got in first.

"Gorse's bridle is dirty," she said with a grimace.

"It needs a good clean."

Sophie shrugged. Sure, she'd only quickly wiped it over, but it wasn't *that* bad. Emily was just nitpicking.

"Hey, do you—" she began, Emily's criticism washing straight over her.

But Emily wasn't quite finished. "And his bed is so messy! Why can't you sweep it up properly?"

That, Sophie reflected, was true. Jack hadn't had time to help her and she'd spent longer chatting to Gorse, and her friends, than she had tidying up.

But before she could say a word, Emily stomped off, her nose stuck in the air. Sophie frowned.

How rude Emily was! Especially as Lainey and Jack were so nice in comparison. She had been hoping to find out a bit more about Fable and whether this sort of thing had happened before. *Still*, she thought, *if Emily was no help, she would have to work it out for herself!*

It was a wonderfully warm evening. The traffic from the main road into town hummed in the far distance and, to Sophie, the yard felt like the most peaceful place ever. Chuckling, she watched as Gorse licked up the last of his feed from his bucket, closing his eyes as if enjoying every last morsel. He seemed relaxed again now, but there was definitely still an odd atmosphere in the stables. More whinnying than usual, and some restless shuffling.

"Come on!" Amina appeared beside Sophie and gave her elbow a gentle tug. "Let's go up to the big field."

Sophie smiled. "Defo," she said enthusiastically. She couldn't *wait* to share her stories. "But let me grab my hoodie."

Running back to the barn and then across to the yard, Sophie paused by Gorse's stable. She had definitely secured the kick bolt in place but, just to make sure, she touched it with her hand. She didn't fancy another boring chore like this afternoon, even if she *had* found out all about Rosie and Fable.

"It's shut," she said, looking upwards at Gorse, who gave her curls a nuzzle, his nose still covered in chaff. "*You're* my witness."

Gorse blew out of his nostrils as if in agreement. Laughing, Sophie planted a kiss on his wide forehead and ran back across the yard and up to the big field, sniffing the air as she caught the delicious waft of a barbecue. This was going to be such a fun night!

"And that," Willow said a little while later, with an elaborate flourish of her hands, "is how we know there is a track ghost!"

Everyone giggled, but huddled together a bit tighter. Willow had just finished her ghost story, about the haunted running track at the local athletics centre where she trained after school. Sophie reached forward and speared yet another marshmallow with her stick. She'd lost count of how many she'd eaten so far and wasn't even that hungry any more, but the melted, gooey marshmallows with their slightly burnt outsides were the most delicious things she'd ever tasted.

"My turn." She grinned and looked around at her friends. "You know I wasn't having you on about those prints, right?"

"Hmmm," Jess said, but she was smiling. "Go on?"

"So," Sophie said, lowering her marshmallow on to the flame and narrowing her eyes. "Earlier today, I was up here. Lainey gave me a job, to clear the field. But while I was up at the hedge, I saw something. Something big. Something *dangerous*."

Poppy, next to her, gave a little gasp and put her hands over her mouth. Even Willow looked a bit doubtful, glancing up behind her as if scanning the hedgerow herself, and the friends huddled even closer together. The ponies in the next field were grazing peacefully now.

"The ponies weren't quiet earlier," Sophie said in a hushed tone. "They were galloping around, trying to get away. They could sense the danger."

Now she had everyone's attention, Sophie couldn't resist embellishing her story, adding a few extra bits that hadn't actually happened. *But they could have*, she told herself with an inner giggle.

"So I crept forward and grabbed the fork, for protection," she continued in a whisper. "I gave the branches a whack, and this horrible creature ran out and up on to the heath before I could stop it. It had *huuuge* teeth. And big red eyes, glowing like the fire."

There was silence, as though everyone was holding their breath. Dusk was falling and Sophie could just make out the mournful hoot of an owl. She'd really scared them now, she thought triumphantly. They believed her!

But then Amina burst into peals of laughter, and so did everyone else. Even Poppy was chuckling.

"Good one, Sophie," she said with a grin. "You nearly had us there!"

Sophie realised she'd gone too far with her story.

"OK, perhaps not *red* eyes," she said hurriedly. "But there was something," she protested. "Something really big and scary in the hedge, just up there!"

"Well, there's a footpath," Jess said in a sensible voice. "I expect it was a dog!"

Sophie glared at her. She didn't want to say there really *had* been a dog.

"But I've got another story!" she said. "Even spookier, and it's totally true…"

"About a cat?" Amina said in a good-natured voice, and after that there was no chance to tell Fable's story. With the spooky atmosphere broken by all the laughter that followed, the moment was gone. Sophie joined in with the chatter but felt a bit annoyed inside. Why had she exaggerated? No one would believe her now. And Fable's story was too special to be treated as a joke.

The rest of the evening passed in a blur of pony gossip and giggles. But, try as she might, Sophie couldn't find the right time to tell her second story. And as the inky dark finally enveloped the pink evening sky, Sophie looked up at the bright and low full moon. Was Rosie up there? Galloping around the fields?

"Come on," Lainey called out cheerfully a short while later. "Bed for you all. You need to have a good night's sleep ready for our cross-country jumping lesson tomorrow."

Sophie gave a little shiver of excitement at the thought of jumping the logs and tyres and water in the cross-country field. Standing up, she stretched and yawned. Her friends did the same. The campfire was reduced to just a few glowing embers now.

"Don't wait for me," Sophie said to Jess as they opened the gate into the yard. "I'm just going to say goodnight to Gorse."

The little Exmoor blinked sleepily as Sophie crossed over to see him, burying his soft nose into the crook of her elbow. Sighing, Sophie placed her forehead against his.

"*You* believe me, don't you?" she whispered. "You always believe me." Gorse wibbled his lip as if in response. Sophie thought about her brothers, and the way they ignored her, and now her friends didn't believe her stories. She supposed it was because they were used to her messing around. But if she couldn't joke around and play pranks, how would she get noticed? Only Gorse stopped her from feeling totally alone.

Patting him one last time, Sophie looked down at the kick bolt, still securely in place. Heading back to the camp barn, she found her steps quickening. The moon had risen higher now, bathing everything in its spooky silvery light. Sophie tumbled into her camp bed, shutting her eyes tightly. Now she'd even frightened herself!

CHAPTER 8

There it was again…

Sitting bolt upright, Sophie held her breath, straining her ears to listen out for what she thought she'd just heard.

Hooves on concrete… She hadn't been dreaming! Something was going on in the yard. The other girls were still asleep. Creeping down between the beds, Sophie opened the barn door just a crack. A whicker sounded through the dark, a whicker she knew so well. It was Gorse! Sophie knew immediately he was asking for her help. She didn't know what for, but she heard it in his whinny. Her heart hammering, Sophie nudged Amina awake.

"Mmmm … what?" Amina didn't even open her eyes.

"Amina," Sophie whispered urgently. "It's Rosie, out in the yard. Fable's mum. She comes every time there's a full moon. I think that's why all the ponies are so spooked!"

Sophie could see that, even half asleep, Amina didn't believe her.

Rolling over, Amina pulled the pillow over her head. "Ha ha," she mumbled. "Go back to sleep, Sophie. You can't fool me again."

And Amina was fast asleep again before Sophie could even blink. She knew the others would say the same too. No one would believe her – *she* wouldn't

have believed her if she'd been them. But something
was out there. She had to go and investigate on her
own. Gorse needed her help!

Taking a deep breath, Sophie crept out into the
yard. The night was still warm, but she was grateful
for the hoodie she'd grabbed from the floor beside
her camp bed. Sophie's eyes took a few seconds to
adjust to the dark. Then she saw it – the outline of
a pony, a pony coming closer and closer and…

Gorse!

Sophie felt a mixture of relief and fear. Gorse was real and right in front of her, but he'd got out of his stable somehow, and Sophie knew why – Rosie!

By now it was clear that the other ponies in the yard were agitated and spooked. There were lots of startled whinnies and the sound of hooves rushing to their doors and back again. Sophie knew she needed to be brave and put Gorse back in his stable. It wouldn't do him any good to be wandering around at night, especially in this frightened state!

Thinking fast, Sophie pulled off her hooded top and wrapped the sleeves round Gorse's neck. Clucking her tongue, she gently encouraged the little Exmoor to head back across the yard to the safety of his stable. Then she'd have to wake Lainey and explain what had happened so they could make sure Gorse's door was completely secure.

"Come on, boy," she said. "I know how you
got out! Rosie let you out!"

But then Gorse stopped dead and snorted,
and the hairs on the back of Sophie's neck
stood up. It was as though every other pony
in the yard was looking in the same direction,
and Sophie felt a shiver of fear. Holding on to

Gorse's thick mane as though for protection, she peered into the darkness. Then she gasped as the reason for Gorse's nerves became clear.

Dragging one leg and slinking low to the ground, the creature got nearer, eyeing Sophie warily. Its fur was a rich reddish brown and its tail was long and bushy. It was a beautiful fox, obviously injured and in trouble!

For a few seconds Sophie just stood and stared. Then she sprang into action. She knew she had to get the fox to a secure area, both to calm the ponies and to make sure it was OK. Looking around her wildly, she gave a triumphant *"Aha!"*

as her eyes fell on the solution — the hay store, straight ahead of her, where she had played so many pranks on her friends. The doors were open — all she needed to do was herd the fox inside and quickly close them.

"Gorse," she said in what she hoped was a calming voice, "I need to get that fox from there —" she gestured at the little animal — "to there." She pointed at the hay barn. Then she gave Gorse a pat. "I know you're frightened, so you can stay here."

Walking towards the fox, Sophie tried to keep her movements slow and deliberate. The creature seemed too exhausted to run.

"Come on," Sophie said quietly as she approached, thinking about all the animal stories on her bookshelves at home. The fox was somehow smaller than she'd imagined them to be. Her plan was working. The fox was backing up now, just a few steps away from the open doors. As soon as it ran in, Sophie would be able to rush forward and close the doors behind it. Then she gave a cry of dismay as the fox suddenly whirled round as fast as it could with its injured leg and started to scuttle back along the length of the stables, heading towards the gate out to the fields. If it got out of the yard, Sophie had lost it, and she knew it wouldn't survive like that much longer.

But just then, there was the scrabble of hooves on cobbles and Gorse trotted a wide circle round, heading the fox back towards Sophie, keeping himself between the creature and the gate. Sophie was too amazed to react at first, then realised Gorse was helping her, as if he understood what she was trying to do. With Gorse blocking its escape into the fields, and with Sophie closing in, the little fox made a dash for the darkness of the hay store.

"Gotcha!" Sophie cried triumphantly, closing the big wooden doors as quickly as she could. Then she turned to Gorse, who had come back to her, and gave him a hug. He had understood her, Sophie was sure of it! They'd worked as the perfect team.

"You're so clever!" she said admiringly, burying her face into his thick mane. "And I'm so glad you're OK too."

It was scary to think about Gorse out of his stable in the middle of the night. There were all sorts of places he could have hurt himself. But he'd been so brave! It was obviously the fox that had been spooking him and the other ponies. That explained the prints, and the rustling in the hedge, and perhaps it had been hiding in the old barrel down by the arena, worrying all the ponies during the gridwork lesson.

Before Sophie could lead Gorse back to his stable, there was a shout and, looking up, she saw Lainey striding out of her house, wax jacket and wellies over her pyjamas, and a worried look on her face.

"Sophie?" she said, getting closer. "What's going on?"

CHAPTER 9

Sophie gestured towards the hay barn.

"It was a fox," she said. "Gorse and I got it in there, but it's really hurt."

Lainey blinked.

"A fox?" she said in a confused voice. "I thought… Oh, it doesn't matter."

Lainey looked a bit wistful. Sophie wondered if she was thinking of Rosie.

"It's injured its leg," Sophie explained. "Quite badly I think."

Lainey nodded, pulling out her mobile phone.

"I have a friend who works in the wildlife centre

out towards the dual carriageway," she said. "They're open twenty-four hours a day so I'll call her now. That was some fast thinking from you. Well done!"

"Thanks," Sophie said, feeling a tiny bit wobbly. The excitement of the fox rescue was just starting to wear off. She leant against Gorse as Lainey made the call.

Eventually, Lainey hung up the phone and smiled at Sophie. "She's on her way," she said. "She was most impressed with the way you'd trapped the fox, and with Gorse's help! But Gorse?" She then frowned. "Was he loose?"

Sophie knew it looked bad.

"Yes, but I promise I shut his stable door properly. I checked it twice," she said all in a rush. "I think it was…"

"Rosie," Sophie and Lainey said at exactly the same time. They looked at each other.

Then Lainey smiled.

"How did you know about Rosie?" she asked gently.

"I met Mary up by the gate yesterday when I was poo picking," Sophie explained. "We were talking and she told me all about Rosie and you bottle-feeding Fable."

Lainey gave a small smile. "Ah, lovely Mary. She was such a help to me back then," she said. "It feels like yesterday, that awful night. But at least I was able to see Fable survive and grow so strong. Rosie was the best pony."

"Does she, Rosie I mean, really visit the yard?" Sophie asked.

"Well," Lainey said, "*I* think so. But she's never actually let a pony out before. I haven't heard anything for years, but the ponies have been acting so oddly these last few days, I did wonder. And with Gorse loose ... well, I just couldn't help but think it was her. They have the same sense of humour so I think they would have been friends." She paused, looking far away. "I was just thinking about her the other week. I kept her horseshoes, but we lost one ages ago. They were engraved. I was wondering about having another search."

Sophie felt really bad. It had to be the horseshoe she and her friends had found and hung on the barn wall when they'd arrived at camp. Rosie, or Rosalina, was the brave pony, and the inscription was about her. It was so sad! She had to tell Lainey the truth.

"I know where it is," she said quietly, and told Lainey about how they'd found it in the dust under the oak tree. "We hung it in the barn, for luck," she finished, hanging her head. "I'm sorry, we didn't know what the writing meant." She hoped Lainey wouldn't be cross.

But Lainey looked thoughtful, and there was a pause.

"Actually," she finally said in a kind voice, "I think that's the perfect place for it. Rosie adored children. She would have loved camp, just like Gorse. Let's keep it there."

They smiled at each other and then, before Sophie could reply, a white van came bumping up the drive. Lainey waved as a woman and a man got out.

"Here's the wildlife rescue team," she said. "We'd better show them where your fox is."

"Whew!"

Sophie yawned and rubbed her eyes. It had taken ages, but the man and the woman from the rescue centre had trapped the fox and put it in a special box for transportation.

"He looks fine," Lainey's friend had explained

to Sophie. "His leg doesn't appear to be broken and we can treat the cut back at the centre. He should make a complete recovery and we can release him again when he's better."

Sophie was really happy she and Gorse had managed to save the little creature. But now she was exhausted!

"You get back to bed." Lainey patted her arm. She had helped Sophie pull a water container over to Gorse's door to keep it extra secure. "It's been quite a night! Come on, I'll walk you over."

But as Lainey opened the door to the barn, Sophie's friends sat up in their camp beds, blinking sleepily at her and looking confused.

"Sophie?" Willow whispered. "What's going on?"

Sophie smiled. "I know you won't believe me, but the most amazing thing has just happened!"

CHAPTER 10

"I can't get over it. After all that —" Amina paused, leaning on her stable fork — "it was a fox spooking the ponies!"

Despite the excitement of the night before, the girls were up early, mucking out their ponies and grooming them, ready for the cross-country lesson that morning.

Sophie laughed. "I know," she said. "Who knew something so small could cause such a commotion?"

Amina laughed too. Then she looked serious. "I'm sorry we didn't believe you yesterday, round the campfire," she said. "And about the prints. You were totally telling the truth."

"That's OK," Sophie replied. "If I hadn't seen the fox for myself, I wouldn't have believed it either! And I did exaggerate, just a *little* bit."

Then she yawned. It had been quite an adventure! The girls hadn't gone straight to sleep after Sophie had come back into the barn. They'd wanted to know every detail about the

fox rescue. She still hadn't told them about Rosie and Fable, but she had brushed her hand over the horseshoe when no one was looking. She'd tell them that story another time. For now, she concentrated on mucking out, making sure the shavings were swept up neatly. She hadn't needed Jack's help today! She'd done a great job by herself, she thought, looking at the tidy stable in satisfaction.

Once everyone had eaten breakfast, it was time to tack up and head over to the cross-country field with Jade. Now the fox had been caught, the atmosphere was calm again and the ponies were all well behaved with no hint of nervousness.

Swinging herself up into Gorse's saddle, Sophie gave him a pat. She'd been looking forward to this lesson all camp. Cross-country was exhilarating and fast and daring; she frowned, thinking of her brothers and what they said about pony riding. If this wasn't a sport, she didn't know what was!

"Brilliant, Sophie!" Jade called. Sophie and Gorse had just flown over a log and were now turning towards a tyre fence and then the drop into water. Leaning forward in the saddle, completely balanced as her hands gave a little on the plaited reins, Sophie felt the wind whip past her cheeks as Gorse jumped perfectly over the tyres. Then on to the drop and, *splash*, into the water they flew, Sophie leaning back as they jumped down, the droplets showering both her and the little Exmoor. This was amazing! Like riding round Badminton! Grinning from ear to ear as she slowed to a bouncy trot, Sophie gave Gorse a hug.

"Wow!"

Sophie looked up as she heard a familiar voice and gave a start. She hadn't expected visitors!

"Mum?" she said. "Samuel?"

Sophie's brother Samuel was dressed in his football training kit. He gave her a wave. As Sophie rode over, Samuel reached his hand out and patted Gorse cautiously.

"We were on the way back from morning training, so I asked if I could stop in and see how you were getting on," Sophie's mum explained. "Brilliantly, I can see!"

"Yes," Sophie said with a smile. "It's been great."

Then she steeled herself for some rude comment from Samuel. Probably something about how riding was boring, or how ponies smelt, or how he hadn't wanted to come. But Samuel was still stroking Gorse, and looking impressed.

"That's actually quite cool, Sophie," he said, and Sophie looked at him in surprise. "I didn't realise you did all that – going fast and jumping over all those big things."

Sophie grinned. "Told ya! But I had to *learn* those things. It's not as easy as it looks!"

"You'll be wanting to try next, Samuel!" her mum laughed, but Samuel looked serious.

"Could I?"

Sophie nearly fell off Gorse in amazement. "They have beginner lessons on Tuesday nights," she said, still unsure if her brother was having her on or not. "If you're serious…?"

"That's one of your training nights," Sophie's mum reminded Samuel, but Samuel shrugged.

"It wouldn't matter if I missed one, just to try," he said, and Sophie smiled at him.

"That's all right with me!" Sophie's mum said, winking at Sophie.

Sophie smiled back with a shake of her head. That was the last thing she had expected! Laughing, she reached down to hug her mum and brother and rode back to rejoin her group. She'd have so much to talk to her grandmother about! And now she'd have her own amazing stories to share.

Sophie put Gorse back into his stable after the lesson, laughing as he wibbled his lip against her hand, hoping for a treat. Giving his forelock a stroke, she thought about what had happened the previous evening. It seemed like a dream now. She hoped the little fox was doing OK. Lainey's friend from the wildlife centre had promised to keep Lainey updated, and Lainey had told Sophie the fox was eating and drinking and already looking brighter. Giving Gorse a final hug, Sophie crossed back over the yard, but stopped, sensing something behind her. Even in the warm sunshine, just for a second, she felt an icy prickle down her spine. The fox was gone. *Could it be…?*

But as she turned round, the sight that greeted her made her laugh out loud. Mini, the tame sheep that Lainey had long given up trying to keep in one place, was pawing at the kick bolt on Gorse's door. It took her a few attempts, but finally her little hoof pushed the bolt down and she gave a triumphant flick of her short woolly tail. Looking Sophie directly in the eye, Gorse then lowered his head and started to nibble at the top latch. He would have been halfway to getting it free if Sophie hadn't stopped him, shooing Mini, who skipped joyfully away.

"I don't believe it!"

Sophie hadn't realised Lainey was in the yard, but she appeared by Sophie's side, a big smile on her face.

"Mini!" Lainey gently scolded the little sheep, who was now enjoying a luxurious scratch against the mounting block. "I knew you were clever, but that's something else. Teaming up with the most mischievous pony on the yard too! We'll have to Mini-proof the stables somehow."

"Do you think that's what happened last night?" Sophie said. "I *know* I checked his door."

Lainey nodded. "Yes," she said. "I expect it was. I reckon Mini's been practising."

"I prefer imagining it was Rosie," Sophie said without thinking. "I'm sure she and Gorse would have been friends, like you said." Then she bit her lip, worried she'd been insensitive somehow.

There was a pause, and Lainey's eyes looked glossy. Then she put a hand on Sophie's arm.

"Do you know," she said quietly, "so do I. Let's go on thinking that."

And then she smiled and carried on across the yard towards Bertie's stable.

Sophie grinned and reached up to pat Gorse. His eyes were merry, as if he'd been caught out. But then Sophie noticed something and peered closer.

There were two hoofprints on the concrete right under his door. The sort Sophie would see on the roads after horses walked past. Gorse was unshod, so his feet didn't really leave marks. Reaching down, Sophie traced them with her finger. There could be lots of explanations she knew. But she had a feeling – something told her these were no ordinary hoofprints.

For a second, she thought about running to tell her friends, to elaborate the story and spook them all after the events of last night. They'd *totally* believe her too. But she didn't need to. She didn't need to play pranks, to be the loudest, or the most entertaining.

All she needed was to be around ponies, to let them tell their stories, to share her own with them. She only had to be herself. So instead she smiled and hugged her beautiful pony close. This was a secret just for her and Gorse.

ARE YOU A PERFECT PONY PRO? TAKE THIS QUIZ TO FIND OUT!

1 WHAT IS THE UNUSUAL TERM USED TO DESCRIBE AN EXMOOR PONY'S EYES?

a) Frog eyes

b) Toad eyes

c) Tadpole eyes

2 WHICH SIDE SHOULD YOU MOUNT, DISMOUNT AND LEAD A PONY FROM?

a) The near side

b) Whichever is closest and most convenient

c) The off side

3 HOW DO YOU KNOW IF YOU ARE ON THE CORRECT CANTER LEAD IN THE ARENA?

a) The inside foreleg will reach furthest forward

b) The outside foreleg will reach furthest forward

c) It doesn't matter about correct legs in the arena, only out hacking

4 WHICH OF THESE ARE <u>NOT</u> A NATIVE PONY BREED TO BRITAIN?

a) The Fell pony

b) The Shetland pony

c) The Konik pony

5 **WHAT COLOUR FLAGS ARE TRADITIONALLY USED ON CROSS-COUNTRY FENCES?**

a) Red and white

b) Pink and neon yellow

c) Lime green and black polka dots

6 **WHAT PLANT THAT GROWS IN FIELDS IS VERY DANGEROUS FOR PONIES?**

a) Blackberries

b) Ragwort

c) Cow parsley

7 WHICH COLOUR IS NOT ALLOWED IN THE EXMOOR BREED?
a) Brown
b) Bay
c) Grey

8 WHAT DO YOU CALL A FOAL'S MOTHER?
a) Sire
b) Dam
c) Colt

9 WHAT IS THE SMALLEST PONY BREED?

a) Shetland
b) Fallabella
c) Dartmoor

10 WHICH OF THESE IS <u>NOT</u> A TYPE OF CROSS-COUNTRY FENCE?

a) Tiger trap
b) Coffin
c) Passage

ANSWERS TO THE QUIZ!

Answers: 1b, 2a, 3a, 4c, 5a, 6b, 7c, 8b, 9b, 10c

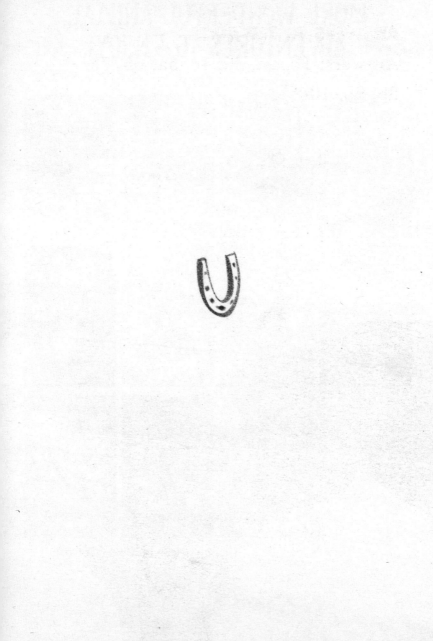

MORE WONDERFUL ANIMAL ADVENTURES TO ENJOY!

Look out for another AMAZING series from Nosy Crow!

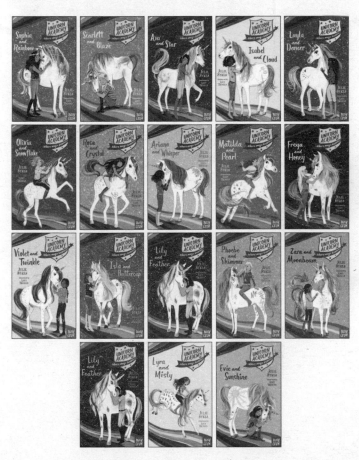